P9-AGF-262

THE
MUSEUM
of
RAIN

McSWEENEY'S
SAN FRANCISCO

Copyright © 2021 Dave Eggers

All rights reserved, including right of reproduction in whole or in part, in any form.

McSweeney's and colophon are registered trademarks of McSweeney's, an independent publisher based in San Francisco.

Cover illustration by Angel Chang.

ISBN 978-1-952119-35-4

10   9   8   7   6   5   4   3   2

www.mcsweeneys.net

Printed in Canada

THE
MUSEUM
of
RAIN

DAVE EGGERS

McSWEENEY'S

"TAKE THEM TO the Museum of Rain," Patrick said.

The family reunion, organized by Patrick to coincide with his seventy-fifth birthday, was in its second day and the adults were catatonic. The bonfire the night before had gone late, and the grownups were hung over, underslept, and emotionally spent. There was a herd of bored kids under sixteen and no one knew what to do with them.

Oisín's mind was empty. "The what again?"

"The Museum of Rain, you senile fool," Patrick said. "You're the one who built it."

Oisín was three years younger than Patrick, but his memory had been spotty since his forties. Museum of Rain. The words emerged from a fog.

"It's just past the mission cemetery," Patrick said. "On that hill overlooking Garza's place."

"I know, I know," Oisín said. "I know where it is. I just needed a minute."

He'd set up the Museum of Rain in the shade of a manzanita tree fifty years ago, a month before he enlisted. It started with a few small jars of California rain. Then, for about five years, every time he was home, he'd add specimens from wherever he'd been—Bozeman, London, Montevideo, Las Cruces. The last one, in a narrow green vase, was from Grenada, where he'd been shot in the shoulder just after landing. That was the end of the invasion for him.

"It can't still be there," Oisín said.

6

"I happen to know it *is* still there," Patrick said. "It was discovered about ten years ago by our neighbors' kids. They said it was actually in decent shape."

"It must be three miles from here," Oisín said. He had no interest in a hike.

"Three point two," Patrick said.

Oisín ate the last scrap of bacon. It had been clinging to his shirt. "You want me to take ten kids on a three-mile hike?" he asked.

"I was just pondering," Patrick went on, "how to occupy some percentage of them for the day, and thought of your thing under the tree. Besides, what else are you contributing to this reunion?" He stood up to signal the conversation had been concluded to his satisfaction. "You want to make some sort of impression on these kids, don't you? None of them have a clue who you are. They think you're some hermit or mountain man. I had to set up this whole weekend. You're freeloading."

This was not remotely true. Patrick's daughter, Evie, was the force behind the reunion. She'd made all the calls, ordered the food, found lodgings for eleven families, forty-four people from eight states and three countries. It was the most elaborate get-together the Mahoneys had ever pulled off. Even Great Uncle Ernst—a German POW who was sent to California in 1943 and never left—had been wheeled in from Stockton. There were three middle-aged relatives from Ireland; no one could figure how they were related to the American Mahoneys, but they added some genealogical ballast. And they'd enjoyed last night's bonfire more than anyone else.

It had been Patrick's idea. In the middle of California, while a swath of Sonoma burned two hundred miles to the north, he insisted on having a bonfire. The kids loved it, and most of the adults, drinking homemade aquavit from an oak cask, grew to accept the fire's existence, as tasteless as it was under the circumstances. The kids had fed it with pieces of a broken-down picnic table, and three Mahoney generations danced around it, rhythmless but free, until Patrick's neighbor, nervous and outraged, flew by at midnight with his crop duster and doused the flames—and half the Mahoney family—with pink fire retardant. That had ended the night.

The family compound was a ramshackle array of Victorians, yurts and double-wides surrounding the original 1845 adobe—bought directly from Don Joaquin Gomez, the Monterey customs officer. In the morning, it looked like an art project gone awry. There were beer bottles, wine bottles, paper plates, chicken bones and skateboards and badminton rackets and a single cerulean sock, and all of it was soggy from the retardant.

Now it was up to Oisín to lead the children away from the mess so things could be returned to some semblance of order for that night's dinner and concert. Patrick wanted to celebrate a distant ancestor, John O'Leary, who had been the right hand and biographer to Simón Bolívar; someone had done 23andMe and the connection, more or less direct, had been evinced. Evie had hired a high school marching band for the party, and ordered an immense sheet cake from Safeway, with an etching of O'Leary replicated on the frosting. Most of the adults had planned to flee to Hoo-ray's, the only bar for eleven miles, until it was over.

"Five minutes," Oisín yelled into the court-yard. He assumed word would get around. He hoped the parents would be motivated to make sure their own children were ready. The round trip would be four hours, minimum—no small gift to all the assembled adults.

"Where's Rebecca?" he asked.

Oisín had rediscovered Rebecca the night before. She was thirteen or fourteen, he guessed, the oldest of Gus and Olympia's three kids. They lived in Malta. Or was it Gran Canaria? Anyway, she'd introduced herself at the bonfire, shook Oisín's hand with firm sincerity, and had answered a series of banal questions with elegance and wit. He'd decided she was the best of the family line, that all of their genetic threads had found their apex in her earnest eyes.

"Here," she said. She'd appeared at his side. She was dressed in army shorts and black sneakers and what seemed to be an Aussie-style cowboy hat. He loved her very much and was sure that together they could map the oceans and conquer space.

"You want a task, Rebecca?" he asked her, knowing the answer would be yes. She nodded emphatically and tilted her head to receive the details of the directive.

"What we need, Rebecca," he said, "is two backpacks. Each with a thermos of water, six apples, a bag of jerky, and some almonds. Not much else. We need them light. Can you manage that?" As he listed the items, and as the significance of the task grew, her face became ever-more joyful. She wrote nothing down but he had no doubt she'd remember every item.

"Five minutes?" she asked.

"Well, four now," he said, and she ran on jackrabbit feet.

"Who's coming?" Oisín yelled into the barn, which in the 1960s had been converted into a dorm for the kids. "Get out here!"

By ones and twos the children arrived, voluntarily or compelled, until he had six.

"Are you Oisín?" said one round-faced boy. "My mom said to find the weird old man wearing a wig." The boy examined Oisín's long white hair as if looking for evidence of its forgery.

"It's not a wig. Who's your mom?" Oisín asked.

"Mary-Frances?" the boy said.

"Your mom should know," Oisín said. "She's got fake teeth and a monkey heart. Tell her I said that."

Two more children, both about ten and squinting in the sun, appeared from the old chicken shack. Oisín thought about sunscreen. He didn't want to get into sunscreen. He hoped the parents would assume him useless on that front.

He scanned the assemblage of gangly youth, looking for anyone he knew. By their ages and his, and because Oisín had no children of his own, he had to assume these were his great-nieces and great-nephews. He recognized one or two of them. One of the ten-year-olds, a densely freckled boy, was named Oisín, too. They called him Oshie. And there were Edward and Ha Yoon's kids; he knew them from their Christmas cards, which arrived each year in late November. The other dark-haired kids he had to guess were from the Ortega side of the family, but then again, the German thread of the family was dark-haired, too. He gave up trying to tie any children to any adults. They were all his for now.

"That it?" Oisín asked.

Two more, a brother-sister pair around twelve years old, appeared from the main house, looking miserable. Both were wearing flip-flops.

"You can be miserable," Oisín said, "but you can't spread it. And change your shoes. Three minutes."

They kicked the dirt and went back to the main house. Oisín hoped they might somehow decide not to come.

"Is anyone scared of snakes?" he asked the group.

There were certainly snakes where they were going—rattlesnakes, too—but along the trail they'd easily see any from a good ten yards away. The local kids knew this.

"Everyone know how to fight a bobcat?" he asked. Oisín had been a camp counselor. This was schtick, a way to get the kids intrigued and maybe more alert, too. He checked his watch. Just after three. They'd walk back at sunset, when the animals would begin retaking the valley. They'd no doubt see deer and lizards and rabbits.

Rebecca returned with the two backpacks. Oisín peered into each. She'd added a bag of dried apricots—Evie's—and a tube of Pringles to one, and a can of Diet Coke and a bag of Swedish fish to the other. But otherwise she'd gathered all the necessary provisions.

"Well done," he said, and patted the top of her Aussie hat. She beamed.

Oisín bounced his index finger in the air above the heads of the assembled children and counted nine. He didn't see the miserable two.

"Now we go," he said, and pointed himself toward the foothills of the Gabilan range.

"Where are we going?" a voice asked.

"The Museum of Rain," Rebecca said with an air of authority.

The miserable two were back. They'd returned, but only one was wearing sneakers. Oisín did not care. Back in the day, he'd done this walk barefoot just to say he could.

The day was gorgeous. Seventy, sunny, with a sleepy haze in the air.

Seeing the party leaving, the last few families readied their own children and sent them to meet the trail. By the time Oisín left the compound and made it around the pond, there were twelve kids. By the time they passed through the gorge there were fourteen.

"Oh shoot," Oisín said. "We don't have sticks. Everybody get a stick."

Oisín had planned this. Another old counselor trick.

"What kind of stick?" the round-faced kid asked.

"Your name?" Oisín asked.

"Declan."

"Okay, Declan. One of two kinds," Oisín said. "The first kind would be a walking stick. That should be as thick as your wrist and as tall as your chest."

Half the kids were already in the thicket, hunting and snapping.

"Either that," Oisín said to their backs, "or a bushwhacking stick. That's for protection if you see a snake or need to fight off a coyote. A bushwhacking stick is about two-and-a-half-feet long, and should be easy to swing around. Like a sword. You have two minutes."

Oisín looked for and found a walking stick for himself. It was a gently bent eucalyptus branch. He stripped it of excess bark and held it away from his eye like a telescope, as if checking the truth of its lines.

The children returned with their bushwhacking sticks and compared them. Many swaps and substitutions ensued, but soon they were ready. They walked on, but then, as they watched Oisín stride magisterially with his walking stick, one by one they traded in their swords for versions of his.

"It's hot," said one girl.

Before her complaint could take hold, the herd's attention flowed to a girl who had a small constellation of blue flowers stuck to her shirt. The other kids wanted to know what they were and how they stayed in place. Oisín knew they were forget-me-nots, but he'd never seen this, the way they clung to clothing. Soon the kids all had powder-blue flowers attached to themselves, too, and they walked on.

They climbed over the Anzas' rough-hewn fence and passed through a wide pasture.

"Aren't there cows here?" Rebecca asked.

"Sometimes," Oisín said. He scanned the valley. "They must be on the other side of the hill. There's shade over there."

"I'm hot," said a voice.

Oisín said nothing. Nothing could be done about the heat, and nothing could be done about children mentioning the heat. But after the pasture there was a winding, marshy stream, and Oisín showed the kids how to wet the backs of their necks with the cool water. The water made everyone thirsty, so Oisín had Rebecca distribute the two thermoses. The kids caught sight of the Pringles in one of the open backpacks and they were quickly devoured.

"Is it true you sit in rivers naked?"

Oisín turned to find a new boy, with close-set eyes and hair like a black mushroom. His mouth was full of chips.

"Who told you that?" Oisín asked.

Rebecca looked up at Oisín. With his answer, her idea of him would either be enhanced or dashed. Though he did indeed sit in rivers naked—his river, behind his cabin, all alone, ten miles from the next human, never seen by anyone—he decided to temper the truth.

"In a bathing suit, yes," he said.

Rebecca's face relaxed.

"I sit in a chair, and the river rushes to me. My doctor told me to do it." He looked down at Rebecca and winked. They walked on, the kids in pairs and clumps, picking up rocks and throwing rocks, examining scat, stopping to empty their shoes of pebbles and dust. A tiny boy was assembling a wildflower bouquet for his mother. Oisín was debating whether to tell him that the beautiful orange flowers that dominated his bunch were California poppies, illegal to pick, when he saw the coyotes.

"Hold on," Oisín said.

There were three of them, about seventy yards away, high on a rounded hill, basking on a wide flat stone. Oisín pointed them out to the children, and soon they were all crouched close to him, whispering and trying to stay still. It had been decades since Oisín had seen coyotes like this, at rest in the sun. This was the closest he'd been to a group—they were so rarely seen in groups. And during the daytime, this was extraordinary.

"What do we do?" asked the boy with mushroom hair.

"Nothing," Oisín whispered. "Just watch. What do you see?"

"They're so skinny," a girl said. Her hair was the color of a pumpkin seed, and she wore rubbery eyeglasses.

"They are, aren't they?" Oisín said. "When we think of coyotes, don't we think of them as fearsome? But they're wiry, smaller than you." He put his hand on the tiny head of the girl with goggle-glasses. It fit perfectly in his palm, like a cantaloupe.

"But it's bigger than the fox," the mushroom boy noted.

There had been a fox the night before, fascinated by the fire, intrigued by the prospect of food scraps. It had circled, casual and confident, for hours.

"The fox was so tiny!" Oshie said.

One of the coyotes lazily raised itself, stretched, and looked in their direction.

"Does he see us?" one of the miserable two asked. She seemed content now that something was happening.

"Probably," Oisín said.

Alone, Oisín would have watched the coyotes for as long as they were there, but he knew the kids would lose patience. Besides, they had only so much light to get to the Museum and back. They marched on, and as they approached the wide flat stone on which the coyotes were sunning, the trio drifted off, disappearing behind the far side of the hill.

"Why do you sit in the river?" another child asked. She had her black hair pulled painfully tight into a ponytail.

"Who are you?" Oisín asked.

"Caitlin," she said.

"For one thing, Caitlin, I like it."

"Why?" she asked.

"It feels good."

"Is the water warm?"

"God no! It's so cold."

Caitlin made a face.

"Is it like a punishment?" she asked.

Oisín laughed. *Catholics.* "No," he said. "It's just something I like to do." Now most of the kids were listening—between the coyotes and Pringles and this story of sitting in rivers, he'd become intriguing, so Oisín decided to tell the plain truth. He would likely never see any of them again, and maybe he could impart this much to them.

"There's a stream that runs behind my cabin," he explained. "Snow from the mountains melts in the spring and comes rushing down, and eventually runs past my home, which is on the valley floor. In the summer, it gets very hot—"

"Where?" the mushroom boy asked.

"Where what?"

"Where do you live?"

"Idaho. Can I continue?"

The boy threw his stick and got another.

"It gets very hot in the summer, and for years I'd been just dipping my feet into the river. And then, about ten years ago, I began sort of crouching down in it, for relief from the heat. But the current is strong, and the river's only about two feet deep, so you can't swim."

"Why not?" This was a new boy, the largest of them all. He was bulbous and heavy-legged and had what Oisín hoped were fake tattoos on his ankles.

"Because it's only two feet deep. It'd be like swimming in a bathtub."

This boy did some calculating and seemed to concur.

"So one day I was sitting in my chair on the side of the river," Oisín continued, "and I was watching the river go by, and it just occurred to me that I could put the chair *in* the river."

"Why?"

It was the same boy.

"You have a habit," Oisín said, "of asking *why* the moment after I *explained* why. It's perverse." The boy slashed a weed with his new stick. Oisín softened his rejoinder with a wink.

"So I sat in the river," he continued, "facing the current, and it was the best of all worlds. The water kept me cool, and I had a comfortable place to sit, and all the while there was the excitement of the river coming at me, over me and through me."

Oisín thought he had painted the picture effectively, and stood with the children in the silence.

"Sounds like you're just sitting in a river."

Oisín looked around for the source of this wisdom. It was the mushroom boy.

"I *am* sitting in a river. That's why I call it riversitting. I invented that word."

"You didn't invent that word," the boy said.

"I did indeed."

"It's not even a word."

"It is. You can look it up."

"Where?"

"Any book. Every book. Every book has some mention of riversitting, and how I made up the word."

Oisín found Rebecca's eyes. She was smiling at him. Nothing better than a child who gets your jokes. He loved her so much it hurt.

They resumed their walk. Rebecca dashed into the thicket and returned with a fuzzy green plant.

"Eat this," she said.

"Fennel?" he asked.

She nodded eagerly and took a bite of hers.

"I haven't had this in so long," he said. The taste was first a delicate mint with a strong licorice chaser.

"Time to eat fennel!" Oisín announced, and he and Rebecca distributed stalks to all the kids. Half of them tried it; the others stood with arms crossed, repulsed.

"You can't just eat random plants!" one of the miserable two said.

"Agreed," Oisín said. "That one, for example, you can't eat." He pointed to a plant he'd just spotted—a spiky fruit called a paddy melon. "But you can eat fennel. And sourgrass. Rebecca?"

Rebecca plucked a handful of sourgrass and distributed it. The local kids knew to suck on the stalk, where the takings were sour, yes, but provided a sugary jolt, too.

"Where are we going?" Caitlin asked.

"The Museum of Rain," Rebecca said.

"It's not a real museum," Caitlin said.

"Yes it is," Rebecca said. "You'll see."

"Is it true you were in a war and got shot?" Caitlin asked.

"More or less, yes," Oisín said.

"But you didn't die?" Caitlin asked.

Oisín laughed. "No, I didn't die."

"So is the museum about the war?" she asked.

"No," he said, "it's not about the war."

Satisfied that there was nothing interesting about Oisín or where they were going, Caitlin skipped ahead to catch up with the larger group.

Oisín slowed down until he and Rebecca were at the rear of the group. The path was dusty, striped by violet treeshadows.

"Sorry about her," Rebecca said.

"So you've been to the Museum?" he asked. She seemed to know more about it than any of the other children.

"No," she said. "But Patrick said it was there. That you built it because you were in love with someone."

Oisín stopped. He didn't know where to start. "Is that something he told everyone, or only you?"

"Just me," she said.

"He's your grandfather?"

She nodded. "Was he wrong?"

"Well, yes. He's usually wrong. The Museum of Rain was just a thing. The words occurred to me one day, and then I started filling jars with rain.

Then I saw a strange hollow in this big old man-zanita. And that became the Museum of Rain."

"Grandpa Patrick said it was a monument to your tears. Because some girl left you."

The kids were far ahead of them now.

"We better catch up," Oisín said. "But listen. Patrick tells a good story. He always has. But it's entirely false. Not a word of it is true. It is, I admit, more memorable than the truth, which is that one day I just did it."

"I like that story, too," she said.

"Sometimes," Oisín said, "people simply do things. They get an idea and do it, and it's not tied up with any love or childhood trauma. If we believe there's a dramatic origin story for every human endeavor, we deprive our species of the ability to simply conjure an idea. To just make stuff and do things."

"I'm learning the banjo," she said, and Oisín laughed a long while.

"You are something," he said, and took her Aussie hat off. He put it on his own head.

"We almost there?" The ankle-tattoo boy had stopped up ahead and was shouting back to them.

Oisín nodded. They were close, he knew, and being closer made him uneasy. He dreaded seeing the Museum, its inevitable and catastrophic decay. Even at its best, it was still just a hippie project, a couple wooden shelves built into a rock, hidden in the overhang of a bigberry manzanita. He and Rebecca had reached the tattoo boy.

"So what, you put some rain in some jars?" the boy asked. "That's what my dad said."

"Basically," Oisín said. And now, he thought, they would be ruinous. Half a century of wind and rot.

They were passing the old cemetery. Oisín knew it was there, but the kids took no notice. To them it would look like a tumble of ancient white stones strewn across a hillside of amber grass. Somewhere in that cemetery, Oisín remembered, were buried Spanish missionaries, Matsun Indians, innumerable cattlemen and cattlewomen, a handful of Mahoneys, one of them an infant, and the man who for thirty years drove the stagecoach between San Juan and Monterey. Now the graves were overgrown and though Oisín knew he should feel wistful, he found he did not much care. It did not move him either way; standing over the dead had never held appeal. Lives were celebrated in stories, not on stones.

But there was a related question Oisín had been ruminating on. What should be preserved? Everything? Nothing? He'd been lugging around

a Colonial-era needlepoint that he'd assumed,
for decades, was worth a fortune. But then, a few
months ago, he'd shown it to a traveling antique
trader and was told it was common and in poor
condition and worth less than $200. Not that
he had ever intended to sell it, but it was a gut
punch. It was the one precious thing he owned.
Everything else in his riverside cabin was plain
and replaceable and would be sold for pennies
when he was gone.

"That's it!" mushroom boy yelled, and then
swerved off the path and up a gentle rocky slope.
Oisín looked up to where he was headed, and
knew the boy had found it. The shape of that
manzanita was unmistakable. The rest of the kids
looked back to Oisín for confirmation. He nodded
and shooed them to follow the boy with the
mushroom head.

"You coming?" Rebecca asked.

Oisín watched the last of the children run up the hill. Half of them had already disappeared in the latticework of the vast manzanita. He expected them to reappear momentarily, complaining about the long walk they'd taken and for what? For some muddy things in an old tree. He looked down on this lovely person, Rebecca.

"You think I should?" He wanted her encouragement. He needed her strength.

"I think we should," she said.

They stepped off the path and made their way up the dusty path cut by the children's scrambling. Rebecca's legs yearned to move faster. Her eyes had already glimpsed some of the activity within the tree. But she stayed with Oisín, matching his deliberate pace. The fact that none of the children had emerged meant something, but Oisín was too preoccupied with completing the climb without having a stroke to guess what.

When they reached the tree, Oisín could hear voices. "Look!" "Open it!" "Over here!" "This one's from Guam!"

Rebecca had paused. From the outside, it looked like an impenetrable thicket emerging from solid rock.

Oisín remembered now that there was an almost invisible entrance, narrow as a cupboard door, on the other side of the rock. He led Rebecca there, feeling dizzy and anxious. For decades he had tried to protect himself from seeing certain things, terrible things that could not be unseen, but he had seen so many, too many, scenes of collapse, failure, villainy. But he had seen great beauty, too. Chiefly in his life, he acknowledged, he had seen beauty. It really was almost all beauty.

"Follow me," Rebecca said. She ducked into the shadows and Oisín followed.

It was glorious, immediately glorious. There were lights. Someone had strung lights throughout and it was as bright as Christmas. Fourteen children were aglow and were examining a multitude of wonders. Hung from every branch there were jars of rain, each of them marked carefully with their provenance and date of capture. San Luis Obispo, 12/28/08. Bend, Oregon, 2/7/12. Maui, 8/8/15. Buenos Aires, 10/16/05. There were a hundred, maybe more, with the light refracted through each, creating the illusion of a vast living chandelier of water and glass.

"Look!"

One of the boys had a book of some kind, wrapped in plastic. He'd pulled it from a gap in the tree's trunk.

"Open it!" Caitlin said.

The boy looked to Oisín for his say-so. Oisín shrugged. No one needed his permission. None of this was his. When he'd last seen this place, it was a dozen jars sitting against the rocks under a tree. He'd hung a sign from the branches, the words MUSEUM OF RAIN burned into a piece of plywood. His creation was little more than that. But now this! Someone, or many people, had grown his humble notion into something gorgeous and delicate and grand.

"Hey!" Another child had found a disposable camera. It, too, was inside a plastic bag. More children gathered around it. They took it out and found a note.

Visitors! it said. *Take a picture of yourselves and please return the camera to the plastic bag. We will develop the film and next time you come to the Museum of Rain, look for your photo among your predecessors. Thx, the Mgmt.*

Oisín looked for a place to sit. He was short of breath. Who had done all this?

"Check it out," a voice said. It sounded like Rebecca. She sat next to him, a stack of photos in her hand. "I think these are people who have been here." The stack was four inches thick.

She flipped through the pictures. There were at least two hundred. People in tanktops— sometime in the '90s? The colors were so bright then. Three young women, hikers, their smiles big, almost overlapping as they squeezed into the frame. A man and his dog. An older couple. A pair of couples. Two teenagers. A rattlesnake!

"Are there snakes here?" Rebecca asked.

Oisín wouldn't have thought so, but yes, there was a photo of a fat rattlesnake taken right there in the shade of the tree. So many photos of couples, families, everyone exuberant, as if overcome with delight to have come across such a strange and unexpected thing.

Oisín looked up, the jars of rain turning slightly amid all the jumbling of the children, the light passing through the water to paint the tangled branches in pale blue and green.

"Another one!"

The mushroom boy gave Rebecca a second set of photos; he'd found it in a wooden birdhouse hung from a high bough. She placed her first stack back in its plastic and they gorged on the second. It was much the same as the first, except the photos were older. These were faded, water-damaged, but the faces had the same expressions of—was it relief?

The faces all seemed relieved to find the world as good as they'd hoped.

Rebecca paused on a photo of a bald woman and her bald daughter, both grinning, eyes bright.

Oisín knew what it likely meant, that the daughter, no more than fifteen, had lost her hair to cancer and the mother had shaved her head in solidarity, that they'd come to the Museum of Rain on purpose or by accident. *Oh Jesus*, Oisín thought. He didn't want to explain it to Rebecca, not now. But her eyes lingered longer on the mother and daughter, and he was sure she knew.

The sun was letting go. To get back before dark they'd have to hurry. Oisín had the kids pack the photos into the plastic bags and return them to the birdhouse and the hollow of the tree. After that there was a complicated process of figuring out whose walking stick was whose, but eventually they all emerged from the tree and into the air and light of the dimming valley.

"Aren't we going to take a picture?" Rebecca asked, and everyone laughed. They'd almost forgotten.

Oisín arranged the children in front of the manzanita and took two pictures, the disposable camera clicking weakly each time.

"Don't you want to be in one?" Rebecca asked. Oisín's impulse was to say *No, no, no*. He couldn't remember the last time anyone had taken a picture of him. Years. Five, ten. There was never an occasion, never a reason.

But now, here and with these children, this was different.

"Okay," he said. He was embarrassed how badly he wanted it.

"I'll take it," said a voice. It was one of the miserable two. She took the camera and stood where Oisín had stood, and Oisín gathered into the mess of squinting children, and in the lavender light, with his arm around Rebecca, he proved that he'd been there.

DAVE EGGERS's recent books include *The Monk of Mokha* and *The Parade*.

ACKNOWLEDGMENTS

The author wishes to thank Amanda Uhle, Mark Bryant, Alvaro Villanueva, Angel Chang, Hannah Tinti, Amy Sumerton, Em-J Staples, Tom Barbash, and VV and AV for their help on this story.

All proceeds from this book go to McSweeney's, a nonprofit publishing company in San Francisco that for twenty-four years has sought to find and amplify new voices.